E
LAN

Lane, Lindsey.

Snuggle Mountain.

DATE			

SNUGGLE MOUNTAIN

by LINDSEY LANE

illustrated by MELISSA IWAI

CLARION BOOKS / NEW YORK

Clarion Books
a Houghton Mifflin Company imprint
215 Park Avenue South, New York, NY 10003

The illustrations were executed in acrylic and Prismacolor pencils.
The text was set in 21-point Advert Rough.

www.houghtonmifflinbooks.com

Manufactured in China

Library of Congress Cataloging-in-Publication Data
Lane, Lindsey.
Snuggle Mountain / by Lindsey Lane ; illustrated by Melissa Iwai.
p. cm.
Summary: In the morning, Emma climbs Snuggle Mountain, trying to rouse the
two-headed Sleeping Giant to make pancakes for breakfast.
ISBN 0-618-04328-4
[1. Parent and child—Fiction. 2. Morning—Fiction. 3. Beds—Fiction.
4. Pancakes, waffles, etc.—Fiction.] I. Iwai, Melissa, ill. II. Title.

PZ7.L2502 Sn 2003
[E]—dc21   2002009035

SCP 10 9 8 7 6 5 4 3 2 1

For Gabriella—thank you for waking me up
—L.L.

For Mom and Dad, who always made
room for me on Snuggle Mountain
—M.I.

Emma stands on her tippiest tiptoes and looks up.
Today's the day she's going to climb
Snuggle Mountain all by herself,
all the way to the top,
and wake the two-headed Giant
who's caught in the Sleeping Spell,
which causes all living creatures,
especially two-headed Giants,
to forget about making pancakes for breakfast.

Emma reaches for a rock to pull herself up.
But the rock isn't a rock.
It moves.
It rises up in a four-legged,
catlike stretch and yawns,
as if it too is caught in the Sleeping Spell.

6

Then it curls up in a crevice
and goes back to sleep.

Emma is halfway up Snuggle Mountain
when she hears a snuffle. An upside-down,
paws-in-the-air, doggy kind of snuffle.
As if a dog is dreaming of crunchy biscuits.
As if it too is trapped
in the Sleeping Spell
and can't wake up.

Lump by bump, Emma inches her way
to the very top of Snuggle Mountain.
Way up here, she can hear
the whispery sighing and
rumbly snoring of the
two-headed Giant.

Snoring is a bad sign.

Snoring means the Giant is deeply asleep.

And if the Giant is deeply asleep,
then Emma must climb into the
Giant's sleeping cave.

And if Emma climbs into that snuggly cave,
then she might get caught in the
Sleeping Spell herself.

Very carefully, crouching atop
Snuggle Mountain,
Emma leans forward
and peers down at the two-headed Giant.
All she can see is its two heads.
One is covered with wild, poked-out hair.
The other has soft, flowing hair.

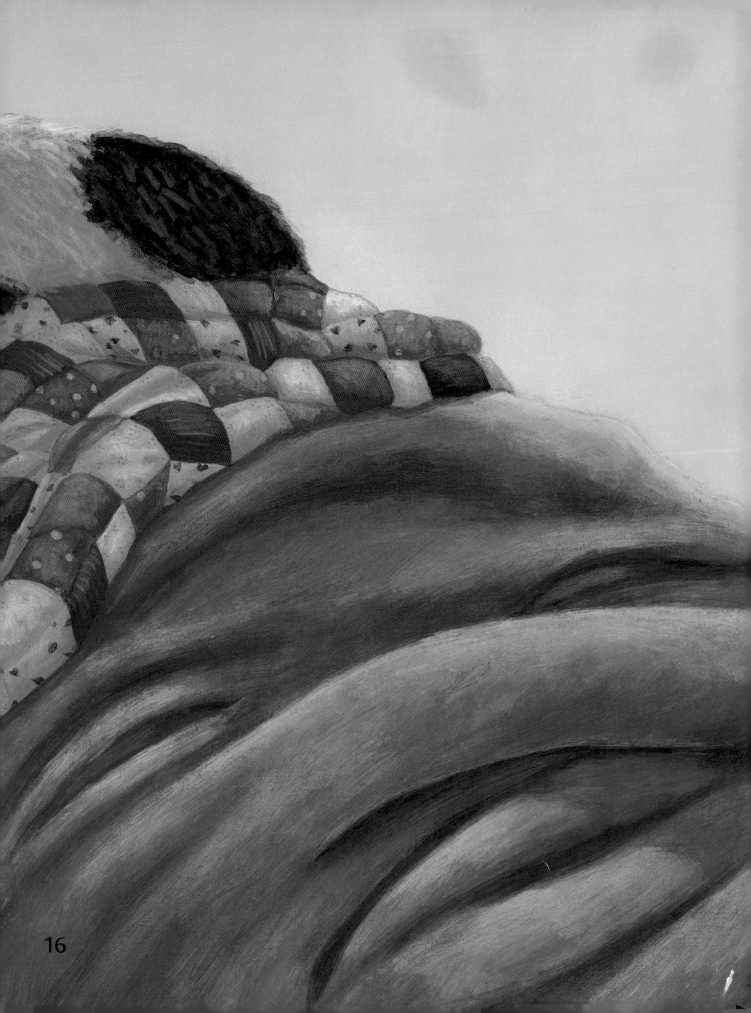

16

"Psst," whispers Emma, and she leans so close
that her hair tickles the Giant's two noses.
Slowly but surely, all four of the Giant's eyes open.
"Wake up," says Emma.

The Giant raises its two heads, moans a great moan, and plops its two heads down again. Before Emma can say another word, Snuggle Mountain shakes,

and Snuggle Mountain quakes.
Peaks become valleys.
Valleys become peaks.
Emma tumbles down Snuggle Mountain
and lands right in front of the
Giant's sleeping cave.

"Hello! Is anybody there?" says Emma,
peeking in just a teeny bit.
Even from the outside, Emma can feel
how warm and cozy the cave is.
She scoots in a little
and tickles the Giant with her toes.
Then she cuddles up next to the Giant.

Before she knows it, she's feeling a little sleepy.

But as soon as she closes her eyes,

her stomach grumbles.

Then it roars.

Emma is hungry.

Gigantically hungry.

She scrambles out of the cave.

She knows what will

break the Sleeping Spell.

"IT'S TIME FOR BREAKFAST!" she announces,
so loud that the Giant pokes its heads
out of the cave.

"Milk!" she yells,
and the snoozing cat climbs
out of her crevice.
"Biscuits!" she shouts,
and the snuffling dog bounds to his feet.

"Pancakes!"
Emma's voice trumpets from the
peaks of Snuggle Mountain,
as Mama and Papa
sit straight up in bed.

Emma leads the charge to the kitchen.
Behind her the cat, the dog,
and Mama and Papa thump downstairs.
She's done it!
She's climbed Snuggle Mountain all by herself
and broken the Sleeping Spell.

Hungry as a mountain climber,

Emma sits at the breakfast table,

watching the pile of pancakes on her plate

grow as tall as Snuggle Mountain.

It's her favorite breakfast in the whole world.

And now that Emma knows she can

climb Snuggle Mountain,

she might have pancakes for breakfast

a lot more often.

31